D0786176

ASTROBLAST!

moon stone mystery

For Nicholas

All rights reserved. Published by Scholastic Inc. SCHOLASTIC, CARTWHEEL BOOKS, and associated logos are trademarks and/or registered trademarks of Scholastic Inc. Library of Congress Cataloging-in-Publication Data is available.

Design by Angela Navarra

ISBN 978-0-545-16926-4

10 9 8 7 6 5 4 3 2   10 11 12 13 14

Printed in the U.S.A. 40
First edition, October 2010

ASTROBLAST!
moon stone mystery
BOB KOLAR

Cartwheel
·B·O·O·K·S· ®

Scholastic Inc.
New York   Toronto   London   Auckland
Sydney   Mexico City   New Delhi   Hong Kong

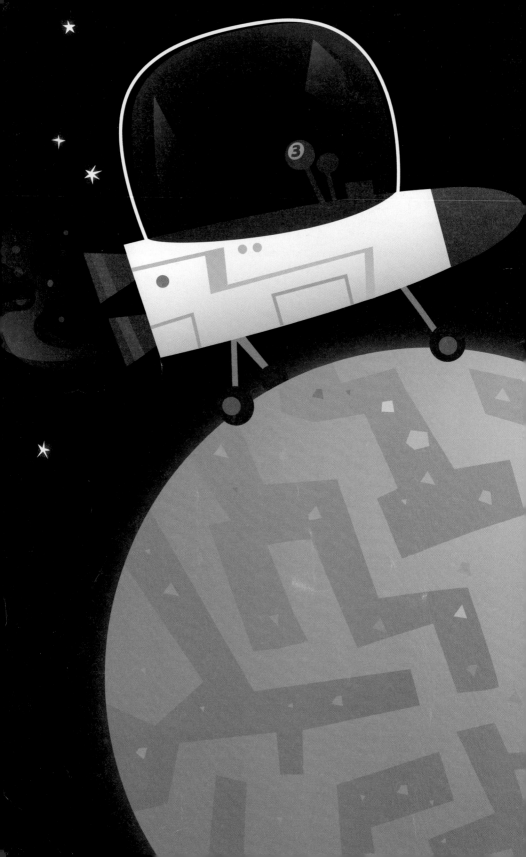

Jet was exploring
nearby the Snack Shack.

He collected moon stones
to put into his pack.

"Rock-tastic!" he said.
"I'll take this one home."

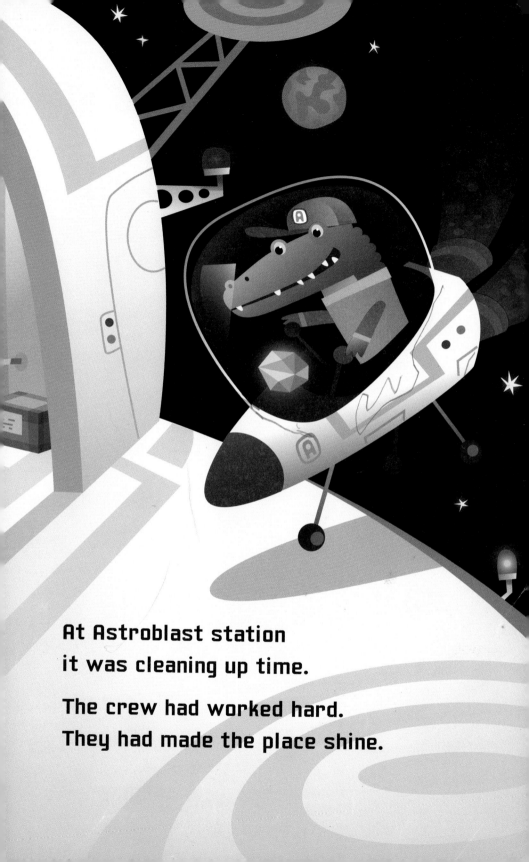

At Astroblast station
it was cleaning up time.

The crew had worked hard.
They had made the place shine.

Then Jet stumbled in and said,
"Look what I've found!"

M is for Moon stone, Mistake, and Mess.

But he slipped and space sauce
spilled all over the ground.

Can you find the letter **M** hidden 7 times in this picture?

Can you find these shapes in the blobs of space sauce?

"Oh, no!" cried the crew,
'cause their shiny clean floor
was sticky and slimy—
not clean anymore.

"Sputnik, you vacuum!"

Can you find the letters that spell out:

YUCKY MESS

The vacuum and mop machines are in a tangled mess.

Can you find more cleaning supplies?

"Apollo, the scrubber!"

Then Radar said, "STOP!"

Gum Remover   Broom   Paper towel   Cleanser

"There's nothing to clean. The mess is all gone!"

The crew was confused. "What *is* going on?"

The floor is so sparkly clean, the crew can see themselves

n it. Can you find 5 things wrong with their reflections?

"Whoa!!!" shouted Jet.
"Something else is not right."

"My once little moon stone
is now big and bright!"

And then...

Can you find these other "bright" things?

A candle   A lightbulb   A lamp   A flashlight   A sun

The giant rock stood
and thanked them a bunch.

"That was a good snack—
now I'm hungry for lunch!"

The crew has some cookies to share with the moon rock.

Can you find them?

The Snack Shack has a new visitor.

"It's not a rock," said Sputnik.
"He's a Snack Shack visitor!"

"I've never seen one like him.
   He's a hungry one for sure."

Can you find 5 things that begin with **V**?

"My mistake. I'm sorry.
I thought you were a stone."

"Now hold on tight," said Jet.
"It's time to take you home."

Jet dropped him off and said good-bye,
but promised to come back,
to bring him lots of goodies from
the Astroblast Snack Shack.

Activity 1

Activity 4

Activity 7

ANSWER KEY

Activity 2

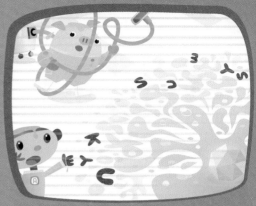

Activity 3

Activity 5

Activity 6

Activity 8

Activity 9

EXTRA MISSIONS

1 Radar dropped his clipboard after the big spill. It's very important: it has next week's menu. Can you help him find it?

2 The mail was delivered to the Snack Shack today. In all the confusion it got scattered around. Where did it all go?

3 Halley loves playing pool. It hasn't been much fun since she lost all of the pool balls. Can you help out the silly rabbit?

4 Every restaurant has lots of things to eat. These were left over from yesterday's menu, but where did they go?

5 The moon stone wasn't the only alien visitor to the Snack Shack today. Did you notice anyone else?

6 Satellites seem to be everywhere. Did you notice these?

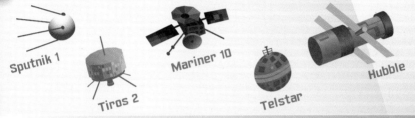

Sputnik 1

Tiros 2

Mariner 10

Telstar

Hubble

7 The Snack Shack is going to have some live music tonight, but only if the crew can find their instruments. They're around here somewhere.

Jet's saxophone

Halley's trumpet

Sputnik's drum

Apollo's accordian

Radar's keyboard

8 Jet loves collecting rocks. Here are some samples he doesn't have yet. Can you find them for his collection?

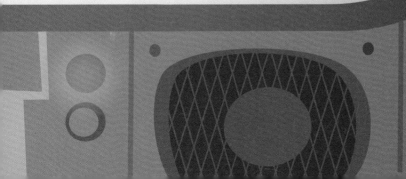